For Michael and Matt,
for being the penguins to my whale.

Special thanks to Mark Sholtez for recording and stitching together
my loose threads of musicianship.

First published in the UK in 2020
by New Frontier Publishing Europe Ltd
Uncommon, 126 New King's Road, London, SW6 4LZ
www.newfrontierpublishing.co.uk

ISBN: 978-1-912858-38-5

Designed by Celeste Hulme and Angie Garland

BLUE WHALE
BLUES

PETER CARNAVAS

One blue morning, Penguin heard Whale singing softly to himself.

'Feeling blue, Whale?'
asked Penguin.

'Look at my bike,' said Whale.
'I don't know which way it goes.'

Penguin laughed.
'Oh, Whale,' he said.
'Don't be blue. It's just upside down.'

Whale felt much better.

But a short time later, Penguin
heard Whale singing again.

'Why so blue, Whale?'
asked Penguin.

'It's my bike again,'
said Whale.
'It's all wet.'

Penguin laughed.
'Oh, Whale,' he said.
'Don't be blue. You can use my towel.'

Whale felt much better.

But later on, Penguin heard
Whale singing again.

'You look blue, Whale,' said Penguin.

'It's my helmet this time,' said Whale.
'I don't know where to put it.'

Penguin laughed.
'Oh, Whale,' he said. 'Don't be blue.
Just put it on your nose.'

Whale felt much better.

At last, everything was ready.

Whale and Penguin hopped on,
                      held on tight
                               and ...

nothing happened.

'Why aren't we moving?' said Whale.

Penguin wasn't listening.
He could see something strange
heading their way.

'What ... is ... that?' whispered Whale.

Turtle said,

'It's a bike.'

Whale slumped to the ocean floor.

'Um, Penguin,' said Whale.
'I don't think my bike is a bike.'

'I think you're right,' said Penguin.

'And, Penguin,' said Whale.
'I think you need legs to ride a bike.
I don't have any legs.'

'I think you're right,' said Penguin ...
and then ...

Penguin laughed
and this time,
so did Whale!

A BIG
BLUE-WHALE-
BELLY-LAUGH!

Ha Ha HA Ha Ha

Whale felt much,
MUCH better.

After that,
Whale forgot all about the bike

and he stopped feeling blue ...

even when
his guitar broke.